Rapunzel Finds a Friend

By Ella Patrick • Illustrated by Jeffrey Thomas

Random House New York

Before Rapunzel knew she was a princess, and before she left her tower and traveled to the kingdom, she was a little girl. And she was very lonely.

Mother Gothel often left her
alone for days. During that time,
the only creatures the little girl
saw were butterflies, bees,
and sometimes a bird or two.

But the butterflies always flittered away.

The bees never got close enough to hug.

And no matter how many
seeds Rapunzel gave them, the
birds never stayed very long.

To fill her days, Rapunzel decided
to take up some hobbies.

First, she tried painting . . .

. . . but her finished artwork didn't
look as good as she hoped it would.

Next, she tried baking . . .

. . . but her cake came out burned and black.

Finally, she tried gardening . . .

. . . but her seeds didn't sprout.

"This stinks," said Rapunzel.

"I can't paint, I can't bake,

and I can't grow

even one strawberry."

Just as she was about to put away her shovel . . .

. . . Rapunzel noticed footprints in the dirt.

"Where did those come from?" she said.

She saw the same
footprints in her paint . . .

. . . and in her baking flour!

"This is a mystery," said Rapunzel. "I love mysteries!"

From then on,
whenever Rapunzel
worked on her art,
she spilled a little paint.

When she baked,
she scattered a little flour.

And when she gardened, she sprinkled a little dirt.

She wanted to see if the prints would reappear.

They always did!

Rapunzel still didn't know who was leaving

the footprints, so she kept practicing her hobbies.

That's how she became so good
at painting, baking, and gardening.

One day, Rapunzel was picking strawberries when she noticed one odd-shaped berry. She reached for it . . .

. . . and it changed color!

A small green chameleon stood

on the windowsill, frozen with fear.

"You must be the one who's been leaving the footprints!" said Rapunzel. The chameleon gave her a tiny nod. The lonely little girl hoped he would stay.

"My name is Rapunzel," she said. "I'll call you Pascal."

Pascal still looked shy. Rapunzel had an idea.

"Would you like some cake?" she asked, holding out a big piece of strawberry shortcake.

As time went by, Rapunzel learned that Pascal never said no to cake. And Pascal learned that Rapunzel was the best friend a chameleon could ever ask for.